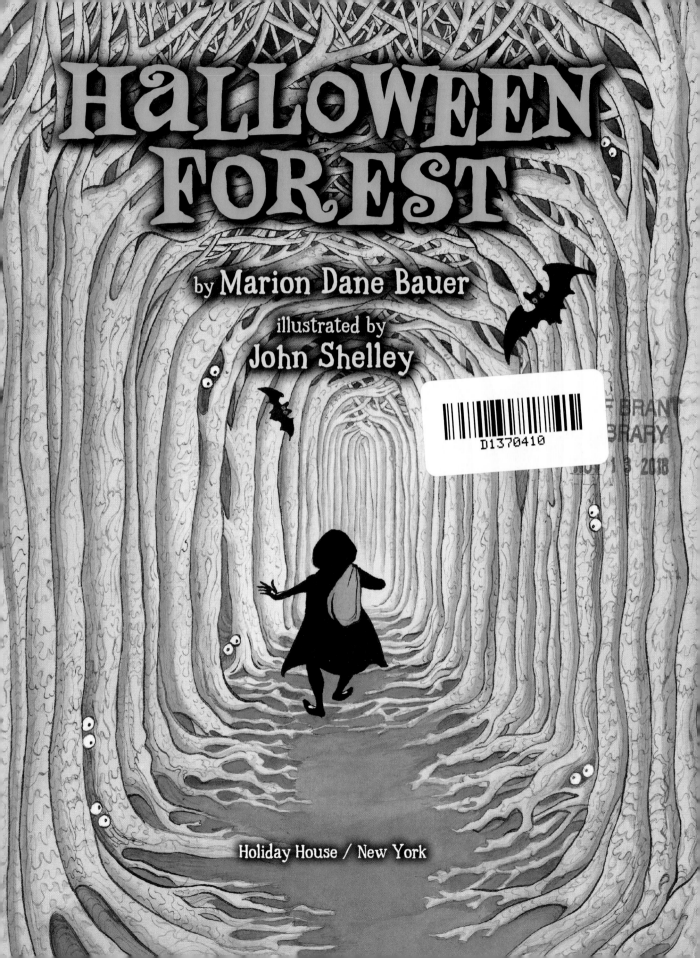

HALLOWEEN FOREST

by **Marion Dane Bauer**

illustrated by
John Shelley

Holiday House / New York

HOLIDAY HOUSE is registered in the U.S. Patent and Trademark Office.
Printed and Bound in May 2018 at Tien Wah Press,
Johor Bahru, Johor, Malaysia.
The artwork was created with pen and India ink with watercolors on watercolor paper.
www.holidayhouse.com
3 5 7 9 10 8 6 4

Library of Congress Cataloging-in-Publication Data
Bauer, Marion Dane.
Halloween forest / by Marion Dane Bauer ; illustrated by John Shelley. – 1st ed.
p. cm.
ISBN 978-0-8234-2324-8 (hardcover)
1. Halloween–Juvenile poetry. 2. Children's poetry, American.
I. Shelley, John, 1959– ill. II. Title.
PS3552.A8363H35 2011
811'.54–dc22
2010029449

ISBN 978-0-8234-4038-2 (paperback)

To all the world's
trick-or-treaters
—M. D. B.

For my shining star,
Seren
—J. S.

Have you ever thrown
your trick-or-treat sack
on your back
on All Hallows' Eve
and taken your leave
of town?

Beyond houses with welcoming doors,
beyond schools and churches and stores,
beyond the zoo with the lion that roars,
what do you think you will find?

I'll give you a hint.
It's not gravestones.
It's not a ghost that
moans and groans.
You'll find a forest
of bones!

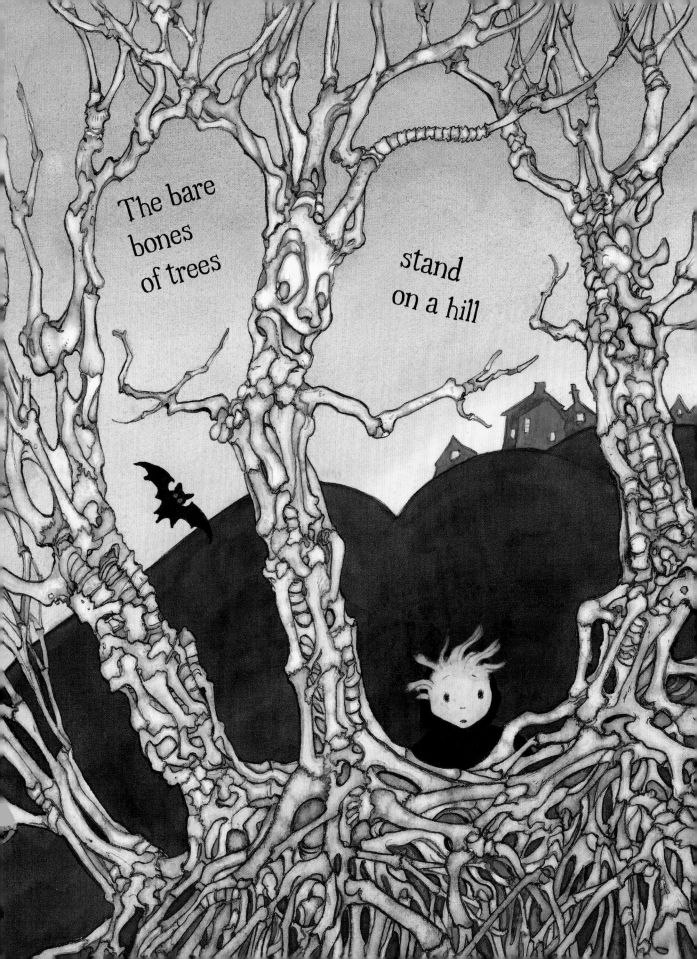

The bare
bones
of trees

stand
on a hill

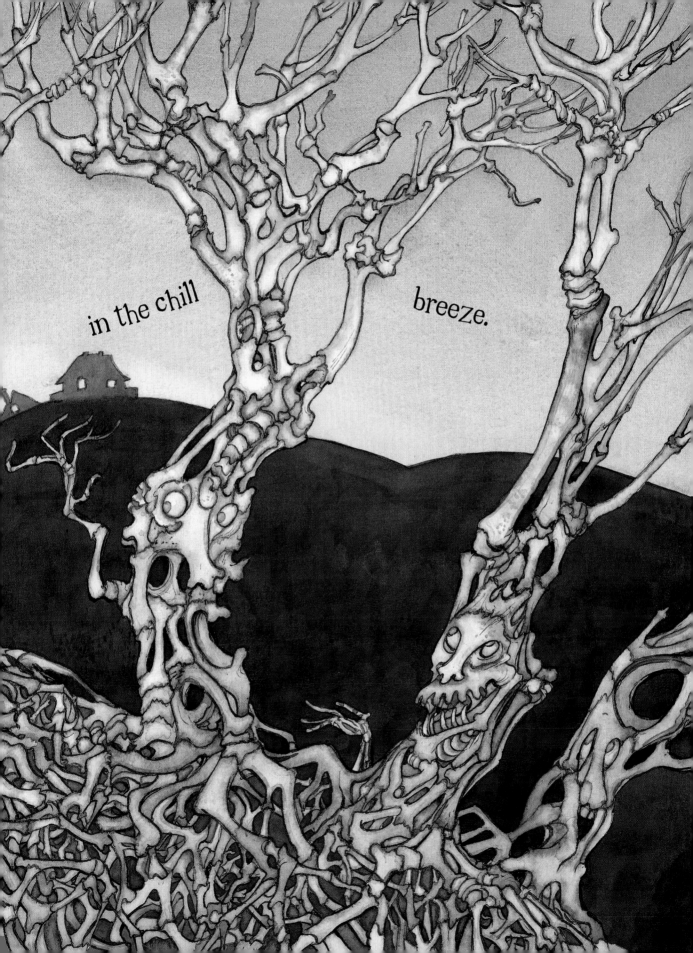

in the chill   breeze.

And hanging from
the branches
are bat bones.
Climbing the trunks
are cat bones.
Snarled in the roots
are rat bones.

Bat bones,
cat bones,
rat bones,
and all are
looking at
you.

There are dog bones

digging up hog bones.

And frog bones

jumping over log bones.

There are even fog bones!

And together they'll cry,
"Take care!
Beware!
Despair!
You can bet
you've just met
your worst nightmare!"

And you?

Will you sigh?

Will you cry?

Will you dash away

in utter dismay?

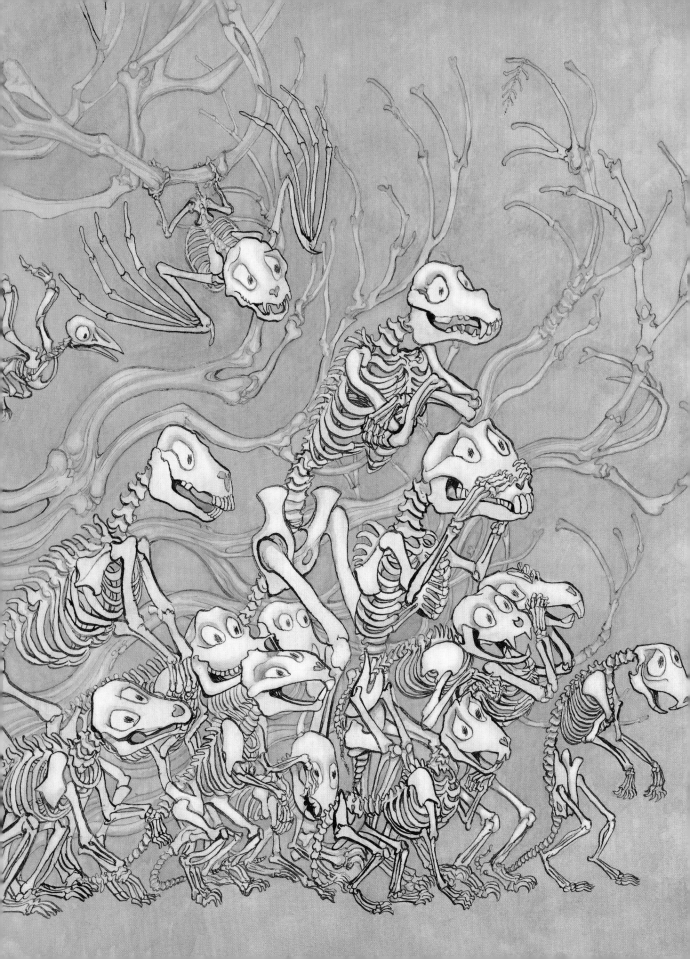

No!
Because you're
too tough
to worry about stuff
like the rattle
and prattle
of bones.

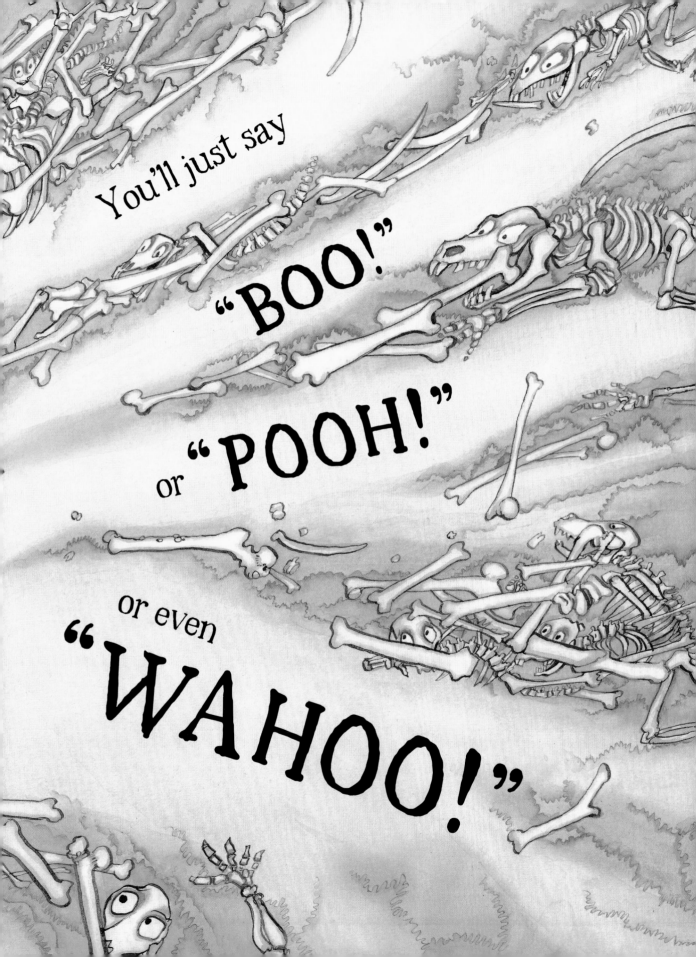

You'll just say

"BOO!"

or "POOH!"

or even "WAHOO!"

while you wiggle

and wriggle

and squiggle

your bones.

Then you'll take
your sack off your back

and hold it out
with a shout.

"Trick or treat!
Smell my feet!

Give me something good to eat!"

And what else
can the bone forest do
but give all its
candy to you?